The Adirondack Kids® #5

Islands in the Sky

To Mikaela,
We hope you enjoy our
Adirondack adventures!
It was so nice to meet you!

The Adirondack Kids® #5

Islands in the Sky

Justin

Gary VanRiper

by Justin & Gary VanRiper
Illustrations by Carol VanRiper

Adirondack Kids Press
Camden, New York

The Adirondack Kids® #5
Islands in the Sky

Justin & Gary VanRiper
Copyright © 2005. All rights reserved.

First Paperback Edition, March 2005

Cover illustration by Susan Loeffler
Illustrated by Carol McCurn VanRiper

Published by
Adirondack Kids Press
39 Second Street
Camden, New York 13316
www.adirondackkids.com

Printed in the United States of America
by Patterson Printing, Michigan

ISBN 0-9707044-5-3

Other Books
by Justin and Gary VanRiper

The Adirondack Kids®

The Adirondack Kids® #2
Rescue on Bald Mountain

The Adirondack Kids® #3
The Lost Lighthouse

The Adirondack Kids® #4
The Great Train Robbery

Other Books
by Justin VanRiper

The Adirondack Kids® Story & Coloring Book
Runaway Dax

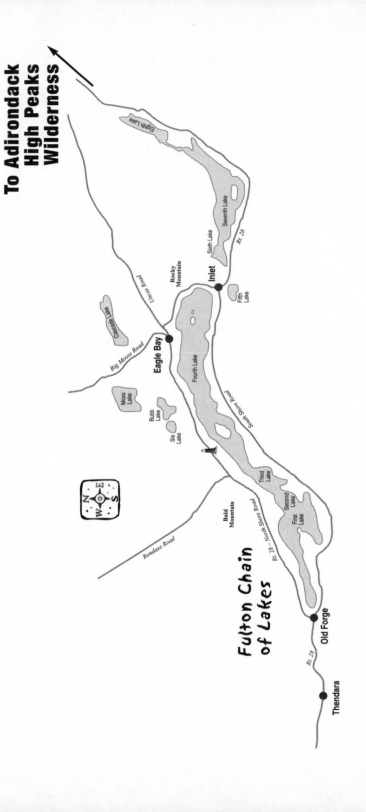

Contents

For Grace Carolyn Ike

first grandchild
first niece
soon to climb the high peaks

There was barking and Dax turned her head. *see page 42*

Chapter One

Happy Trails

Justin Robert took his time signing the register at the Heart Lake trailhead. The end of his tongue stuck out and curled around the corner of his mouth. He was concentrating. It would be important to write down all the information in the book clearly and correctly in case he and his hiking companions were lost or needed help.

"Hurry up," said his friend, Nick Barnes. "My pack is killing me."

Justin ignored him and kept on writing. There were **4** people in their group and they would be on the trail for **3** days. He jotted the numbers in the designated boxes on the page.

"That's it, I'm taking this thing off," said Nick. He unstrapped his green backpack that contained a food canister, dropped it to the ground, and sat on it. "Let us know when the story you're writing is all done."

Jackie Salsberry pulled her blonde hair back into a ponytail as she reviewed all the information pinned up on the inside walls of the small kiosk that housed the register. There were maps and posters and camping

Justin Robert took his time signing the register
at the Heart Lake trailhead.

instructions with stern warnings. Most of the information she already knew. But she still read everything, even what was written in her favorite second language – French. "Hiking in the Adirondack high peaks is really serious business," she said, and turned to face her two summer best friends.

Nick seemed totally uninterested and remained sulking and sitting on his pack. Jackie shook her head. "If you knew how to wear that thing, you wouldn't even know you had it on," she said.

Nick cocked his head and smiled with a closed-mouth grin that said, 'Not funny.'

Justin had stopped writing and stared at the next question in the register. He was stuck. Destination? He knew where they were going. He and his friends had been planning this trip for two weeks. He just hoped he could spell it right. **Algonquin**, he wrote, and then hopped off a second food canister he had used as a stool to reach the book. "Finished!" he announced.

"Good timing," said Jackie. "Here comes your grandfather."

Grandpa Robert was moving from the Information Center across the busy parking area to join them. His long, sturdy strides took him quickly past open-backed vans and SUVs parked along the outer edges of the lot. Hikers of all ages and sizes were yanking out their gear – some sitting to pull on wool socks and waterproof boots. As tall as he was, the morning sun reaching over the trees caught only the top of his backpack that seemed to tower above his graying head. "All set?" he asked.

"Aren't you going to check the trail register and make sure I filled it out all right?" asked Justin.

"I am sure you did fine," said his grandfather.

That was one of the things Justin liked the best about his grandfather. He always seemed to treat him, even at ten years old, more like a grown-up. But that also made him feel a certain pressure to want to do things right and never disappoint him.

"Excuse me." A small band of hikers emerged from the woods. The leader stepped into the open kiosk to sign his group out on the trail register. He looked upset.

"Where is your pack?" Jackie asked.

"That's something we wanted to tell you and anyone else hiking this weekend," said the young man. He took off his wide-brimmed hat and ran a bandanna through his sweaty, sandy-colored hair. "Be careful out there. A pushy bear cut our trip short. A very bold one. We used a canister to protect our food, but he caught us off guard – raided us right at dinnertime and got everything – tore my pack to ribbons."

He picked up the pencil and flipped back through several pages of the register to find his group. "There we are," he said, and made a check mark to sign out. "We're going to report the bear incident right now." Then he ran to catch up with his buddies who were already halfway across the parking lot.

4

Nick stood up, stared down at his pack and pointed at it. "There is no way I am carrying this canister," he said. "Why am I the one stuck carrying all the food?"

Jackie corrected him. "First of all, you are not the only one carrying food," she said. "And second, you are the one who insisted on carrying as much food as you could."

Nick frowned. "That was before I knew that giant bears were out attacking everybody."

"Well, Justin is carrying a canister and it doesn't bother him," Jackie said. She helped him strap the black, plastic container onto the back of his pack. "Right, Justin?"

"Um, right," said Justin. He managed a weak smile. Then it occurred to him someone was missing. "Hey, where's grandpa?"

The mouth of the trail was still in deep shadow. They all looked just in time to see the back of Grandpa Robert suddenly disappear into the dark woods.

"Let's go," said Justin. Boots pounding and back-packs jiggling, he and Jackie hurried to follow him.

Nick struggled to pull his pack back on as he stumbled off after them. "Hey, wait up," he said, and briefly knelt to adjust one of his socks. "Bears don't eat people, do they?" He stood and ran to catch up. "I'm walking in the middle! The bears will get you before they get me!" And in a moment, the woods had swallowed him up, too.

Chapter Two

Off to See Algonquin

It didn't take long for the fear of bears to fade as they moved along the wide path and took in the grandeur of the mighty Adirondack forest.

Nick had already even hustled into the lead. "Hey, this is fun," he said, as he bounced along the planks of a man-made bridge. "This is sure a lot easier than climbing Bald Mountain back at camp."

Nick was wrong. Justin knew it. He saw his grandpa struggle to hold back a smile. Then he looked from side to side as he marched ahead, wondering why the trees seemed taller here than back in Eagle Bay. *It's still the Adirondacks,* he thought. *But it feels a lot different.*

Jackie strode up alongside him. "The high peaks wilderness is incredible, isn't it," she said.

Justin nodded. "So, are you disappointed you aren't getting to climb Mount Marcy first?"

Jackie vigorously shook her head. "Are you kidding?" she said. "It would be awesome to climb New York State's highest peak first. But just to be here, to climb any high peak at all, is the greatest thing ever."

6

The woods seemed different. Now Jackie seemed different. She was always full of energy. But Justin could not remember a time when she looked and sounded so happy.

"Ouch." It was Nick, sprawled out face down on the trail. With the green pack on his stocky back, he looked like a big turtle crawling along as he struggled to stand. "Stupid rock," he said.

At least some things never change, thought Justin. He and Jackie bent over to help their friend get up.

"The trail is wide enough for all three of us to walk side by side," said Jackie. "Here, lock arms with me."

Before Justin and Nick knew what was happening, she was pulling them along and quoting lines from The Wizard of Oz. "Lions and tigers and bears, oh my. Lions and tigers and bears."

Nick pouted. "Why did you have to remind us about the bears," he said. He began looking at every large tree with suspicion, as if each one was concealing a ferocious beast just waiting to pounce on him.

"Let's sing," said Jackie.

"Are you crazy?" said Nick.

Justin pulled back and shook his head. "What's wrong with you?" he asked.

Jackie jerked them forward. "Keep moving," she said; and before the boys could protest, she broke into song. Instead of singing, "we're off to see the wizard," she sang, "we're off to see Algonquin." She stopped and looked at Justin. "Hey, all we're missing

7

now is that little dog, Todo. It's too bad Dax isn't with us, even though she is a cat."

"At least we're not missing the wicked witch," said Nick, as he glanced over at the only girl among them.

Jackie scowled at him.

"That's scary," said Nick. "If you were green, you'd look just like her."

Jackie pointed at Nick. "Oh, look," she said. "It's a scarecrow." She sang again. "If you only had a brain."

Justin wasn't smiling. He wasn't even paying attention any more. For a while he had not thought about his calico companion. He had wanted to bring Dax on the trip so badly, but it just wasn't possible. And with mom and dad in Lake Placid writing and taking pictures for a story about Olympic skiers, there was no one at camp to take care of her.

"What's wrong, Justin?" asked Jackie.

"I was just thinking about Dax," he said.

"I'm sorry," Jackie said. "I shouldn't have mentioned her. I am sure she is fine."

Nick chimed in. "Yeah," he said. "You know how much she loves hanging out in your boat? I'll bet she's sleeping in the kayak in the boathouse right now."

Nick was only partly right. Dax was in a kayak. But not in Justin's kayak. And not in the boathouse. And she definitely was not sleeping.

Chapter Three

An Unplanned Vacation

Dax stood up on her hind legs in the kayak and rested her front paws on the edge of the cockpit. She peered out over the bow of the boat. The wind blew with such force it pressed her whiskers back fully against her face. She had ridden on a jet ski in Fourth Lake and on a skateboard in North Creek. And she had taken many rides in a kayak before. But never this fast.

Of course, she had never been riding in a kayak on top of a jeep moving down Route 28 at 55 miles per hour before, either.

It was the kayak strapped on top of the jeep at the ice cream stand in Eagle Bay that had caught her attention while she was out searching for Justin. The long, green craft looked exactly like the one stored in the boathouse back at camp.

It only took one leap for Dax to reach the hood of the jeep. A second leap took her to the roof. One more and she landed smack dab into the middle of the seat of the boat. Each move was quiet and smooth.

She had very little time to investigate the dark caverns of the bow and stern of the kayak, when both the jeep and boat shook with two loud slams. Human passengers were now below. The engine rumbled to life and the vehicle began to move. Slow at first. And then a little faster.

In moments the jeep was on the main highway and had zoomed past the camp driveway and on into the hamlet of Inlet.

Then it was past the small shops and sidewalks full of tourists. Past the library and the church. Past Fifth Lake. There the vehicle picked up even more speed.

That was when Dax stood up on her hind legs and lifted her head into the blast of fast-rushing air. Her eyes narrowed. She could not read, of course. But if she could have, she would have read the back of the hamlet's welcome sign: Thanks for Visiting – Come Again Soon.

Chapter Four

Spishing

The four steady hikers had left the Blue trail at about one mile, and were now on the Yellow trail. As the sun rose, so did the temperature.

Nick was huffing and puffing. There were no more jokes. And he was no longer in the lead. Neither were Justin or Jackie.

Grandpa Robert now led the way with a slow and even pace, his long legs helping him pick his way up, over and around the many small rocks and boulders and broken branches that now cluttered the narrowing trail. A pair of trekking poles helped him maintain his balance as he moved on.

"Are we lost?" asked Nick. "Where did the trail go?"

"We are on it," said Justin.

Nick grimaced. "All these rocks are the trail?" he said. "When do they end?"

"They don't," said Jackie, in an even tone. "They just get bigger."

Nick groaned.

Justin's mouth was dry and he smacked his lips. The smell of wood was in the air. "The inside of my

11

mouth tastes like a popsicle stick," he said.

"Don't talk about ice cream," said Nick. "I'm hungry – and thirsty."

Grandpa Robert stopped and eased his backpack down onto a boulder. "Let's all have some water," he said. "We don't want anyone to dehydrate."

As the three Adirondack kids tipped their heads back to drink deeply from their water bottles, they heard a strange sound issue from the mouth of Justin's grandfather.

"Is he all right?" asked Nick. "He sounds like a popped tire gushing out air."

"Be quiet and listen," said Jackie. "He's spishing."

Nick looked around. "In the middle of the woods?" he asked. "And without a pole?"

"Not fishing," said Jackie, who knew exactly what Grandpa Robert was doing. "He's spishing. It's a sound you can make that attracts birds. If they are hiding, sometimes you can get them to come out and check the noise. No one knows for sure why it works – it just does."

Grandpa Robert made the sound again.

"I hear birds," said Justin. He pointed into the forest canopy. "Look, there they are."

Two black-capped chickadees were taking turns flitting from branch to branch, inching their way toward Justin's grandfather. If he had reached out, he could have nearly touched one.

"That is so cool," said Nick. "Let me try." He began moving his head around and spitting with abandon in every direction. The fact that he had just taken a large swig of water only enhanced the showering effect.

"Watch it!" said Justin. He ducked, but not before suffering a direct hit in the face from his friend who was functioning more like a broken lawn sprinkler than a bird caller.

Even at twelve years old, Jackie was nearly a master birder herself. She could already identify nearly every bird in New York State and knew a lot of ways to get close to them. "You are supposed to go, *spish-spish-spish-spish*," she said, trying to help Nick. "Not, *spit-spit-spit-spit*." She wiped off her forehead. "It's like making a *shh* sound, but with an *sp* in front of it. Like this." She demonstrated it perfectly.

Nick still couldn't get it. As he continued to struggle, Justin and Jackie moved out of bathing range.

"I think I can do it," said Justin. He took a deep breath and then repeated rapidly the airy spishing sound three or four times as best as he could. He noticed Jackie and Nick and his grandfather all pointing toward the trees behind him. Then he felt a funny, tickling sensation through the top of his red bucket hat.

"It's another chickadee," said Jackie, smiling. "Don't move."

Justin froze. Not because he was scared, but because he could feel the feet of the tiny bird dancing about on his head and wanted it to last as long as possible. He moved his eyes upward until they crossed, but

13

Justin could feel the feet of the tiny bird
dancing about on his head.

14

still could not catch a glimpse of the songbird's ballet.

Almost as quickly as the performance began, it was over.

Grandpa Robert strapped on his pack and began moving forward again.

A cool drink of water and short rest with a private woodland show. Their enthusiasm revived, the Adirondack kids adjusted their own packs and followed him with new energy up the rocky Yellow trail.

Chapter Five

Dax on Display

Dax was born in the Adirondacks and had lived on Fourth Lake with Captain Conall McBride of the mail boat, *Miss America*, until Justin had adopted her.

Of course, everyone at camp said it was Dax who had adopted Justin. The two had been inseparable all summer, but now her quest to be reunited with her favorite human companion was actually leading her farther and farther away from home. She had traveled many times by mail boat from Fourth Lake to Old Forge Pond and back again, but had never traveled that distance in a car before.

As the jeep Dax was riding on continued along Route 28, she lay napping in the bow of the boat. Wind created by the speeding vehicle caused the nylon straps holding the boat on the roof to buzz. It was like sleeping inside of an active beehive. But Dax didn't seem to mind. It was dark and secure and the steady hum was more of a comfort than an irritation. She did not wake up until the jeep sharply turned, causing her to roll off her mattress and bump against the wall.

There were two slams and she popped her head back up through the cockpit in time to see the jeep's two passengers walking hand in hand toward a large building.

The Adirondack Museum at Blue Mountain Lake had thousands of visitors every year. But not many were cats. Dax was out of the boat and onto the pavement in seconds, and with so many tourists moving in and out of the building, easily slipped through the front door.

She turned right, ignoring the 32-foot racing sailboat that hung suspended from the ceiling in the main foyer of the museum's Visitor Center. Then she pranced left of the Gift Shop, past the ticket counter and out onto the main grounds.

The Whiteface Fire Tower looked familiar. Dax had been up such a tower once before – on Bald Mountain. She was considering climbing the one in front of her, when a small group of young children rushed by. To avoid being trampled, she darted aside and then decided to follow them.

The short chase led to the boat building where a tall bearded man in a red-and-black checkered shirt stood perfectly still, holding a huge guideboat over his head. Dax abandoned the running children and jumped to the guide's feet. She sat down and looked up at him.

"Hey, look at the kitty in that exhibit," said a man to his daughter. "Doesn't she look real?"

A museum official heard the comment, glanced

over and saw the motionless calico cat sitting at the feet of the mammoth manikin guide. A confused look came over her face.

Then the cat moved. Then so did the official. Dax could sense the human's fast approach and she moved quickly back the way she had come. Off the main grounds she ran, back into the Visitor Center, around the ticket counter, past the sailboat and out the front door.

A small cavern lay in front of her. Bounding down the cement steps and onto the sidewalk, Dax lunged into the small cave and crouched behind several large objects inside to hide.

She peered out into the light and saw two legs near the entrance of her hiding spot. Then two hands appeared and pushed a good-sized object into the cave toward her. Then another. And another. Her personal space was shrinking quickly and soon her view to the outside world was nearly completely blocked. There was a loud squeak and bang. Everything went black.

The entrance to the cave was closed.

Chapter Six

Setting Up Camp

"Look at all the litter," said Justin, who was staring downward more than upward as he carefully picked his steps along the boulder-strewn trail. "There's paper on the ground everywhere."

"That's not litter," said Grandpa Robert. "That's from paper birch, probably the most common hardwood tree in the high peaks."

Nick shook his head. "So it is okay for nature to litter, just not people," he said.

Nearly four hours had passed since signing in at the trailhead.

Some hikers rushed past them on their way up the trail and others descended slowly, occasionally stopping for a quick breath or drink of water. So far along the way they had met people not only from the State of New York, but also from Vermont, Virginia, Canada and even Iceland.

"When are we going to get there?" asked Nick. "My pack is killing me."

"We're here," said Grandpa Robert.

The answer so startled Nick, he stood with his

mouth wide open, not knowing what to say. He had been all prepared for at least four to five more minutes of constant complaining.

"You can close your mouth now," said Jackie. "Unless you like swallowing mosquitoes."

A thin, brown sign made of wood and bearing in yellow paint the word, campsite, was tacked high on a tree. It was there they entered the forest.

Pitching their tent in the small clearing some 40 feet off the main trail was an adventure in itself.

Nick kept trying to engage Justin in a sword fight using the tent poles. When his tent pole was taken away, he picked up one of Grandpa Robert's trekking poles and continued poking at his friend.

"Stop it, Nick," said Jackie. "We have a lot of work to do. Leave Justin alone."

Nick looked disappointed. "What's the matter with you, Justin?" he asked. "You're no fun anymore."

Justin half ignored him, and looked over at his grandfather who continued working steadfastly to set up camp. "Not now, Nick," he said firmly, and then whispered, "we'll play later."

With Nick under control, the gold nylon tent popped quickly into shape.

"It looks like an Egyptian pyramid," said Nick.

"Let's put in our sleeping bags," said Justin. He unstrapped his bag from the outside of his backpack, unzipped the front door of the tent and crawled in. "Hand me your bag, Nick."

"No way," said Nick. "I'm exploring the pyramid

with you." And in he went, hauling his sleeping bag with him.

Jackie gladly tossed her bag in behind him.

"Hey, that hurt," said Nick from somewhere inside the tent. He stuck his head out of the door, grinning. "Just kidding."

Justin pushed him out of the tent and ran over to his grandfather who was fastening a line between two trees. "I think we are in trouble," he said. Jackie and Nick joined them. "There is only enough room in the tent for three sleeping bags."

Grandpa Robert smiled. "That is why I brought this," he said. He tugged slightly on the line which opened into a small net.

"It looks like a hammock," said Nick.

"It *is* a hammock," said Grandpa Robert. "You three will be sleeping in the tent. And I will be sleeping like I usually do out in this gorgeous wilderness – in the open air and under the stars."

Jackie frowned. "Look," she said. "Someone took a jackknife to one of these trees." She ran her fingers inside several vertical gashes cut into the bark.

"That's just not right," said Justin, shaking his head. "It was probably someone trying to carve their name or a date they camped here or something."

"But the letters are huge," said Nick. He could place two of his own fingers side by side in each crevice. "Look how wide and deep they are."

"No person made those marks," said Grandpa Robert.

Grandpa Robert told them the last thing they wanted
to hear. "Those gashes were made by a bear."

Puzzled, the three Adirondack kids looked up at him. Then he told them the last thing they wanted to hear. "Those gashes were made by a bear."

Chapter Seven

Heart of the Adirondacks

The Adirondack tour bus pulled away from the curb of the museum with an unaccounted for passenger. A stowaway. Dax's safe hiding place had suddenly become a prison on wheels.

As the grand silver coach turned onto the highway moving northward and wound its way around Blue Mountain, a host of the packages and suitcases in the baggage compartment began to shift.

While all 40 passengers were resting above in comfortable chairs, reading books, sipping on sodas or dozing off, Dax was below, fighting with every bend in the road for her very life.

Superior vision in the dark was helpful. And she was masterful at moving, as cats can be, and somehow avoided being squashed, despite the tight quarters and constantly heaving luggage.

It wasn't the final turn, but the final stop that nearly got her. As the bus came to an abrupt halt, the baggage didn't.

Even good-natured cats have their limits. Dax let out a harsh *meow* as two suitcases collided and squeezed her already slender body. It would not be the last time she would cry out during her involuntary cross-country adventure.

Someone above must have heard the chilling shriek even over the sound of the idling engine, because moments later the compartment door was swung open. Dax's eyes were still adjusting to the daylight when she darted out of her sheet-metal jail. There were no outstretched hands to grab her. After all, pets were not allowed on the tour bus.

Dax crouched under a candy-red van in the parking lot while people exited the bus and stretched their legs at the Town of Newcomb Public Picnic Area.

The Heart of the Adirondacks. That is what it said in bold gold letters on the face of a stone monument that overlooked a wide section of the high peaks region.

A piece of plexiglass acted like a window in the center of the unique display. It was specially cut and etched along the top to repeat the contour of the mountains that lay off on the horizon. Each distinct curve in the glass matched a distant mountain peak and had a letter of the alphabet stuck on it. The names of the mountains were listed alphabetically on square white tiles on a shelf below.

It was an incredible view and most of the humans gathered there were squinting, pointing at the glass and then looking down at the names printed on the tiles in an attempt to successfully identify each mountain.

Twenty minutes later, the bus reloaded and rumbled

off, and it was Dax's turn to explore the display. She left the protection of the candy-red van and walked out onto the brown brick sidewalk leading up to and surrounding the unique monument.

Always seeking the highest point to perch, she sprang onto the shelf with the square white tiles. Walking casually from left to right and from tile to tile, her paws touched some of the letters of the alphabet and the names of the mountains recorded next to them. A – Santonini. C – Henderson. F – Hedgehog. G – Marshall. She sat for a moment to bask in the sun and lick her paws on I and J – Skylight and Algonquin.

She was surprised when a small girl gently picked her up and whispered into her ear, "Shhh."

Chapter Eight

Get Out of the Woods, Now!

Suddenly the wide, vertical gashes found up and down the tree trunk didn't look like letters or numbers at all. They were giant exclamation points. The Adirondack kids provided the imaginary sentences. Bears are here! Go home! Get out of the woods, now!

"Let's get out of here!" said Nick. He started marching back toward the trail. "And I am not taking my pack. Not with all that bear food in it."

Justin and Jackie looked at Grandpa Robert for reassurance. They were not disappointed. "This campsite is used all the time," he said. "Bear attacks are very, very unusual. In fact, more people are injured in the wild by rabid raccoons or skunks."

"Do you mean we have to worry about *crazy* animals, too?" asked Nick. "What do the skunks do? Just run up to you and start squirting you for no reason?" He moaned and started chanting. "Why did I come? Why did I come?"

Justin wasn't quite sure what to think about the bears. He remembered hearing about the one that had walked into the back door of the Tamarack

27

Theater back at camp in Inlet.

Right in the middle of the movie, the bear lumbered straight up the center aisle, out into the lobby and buried his head in the popcorn machine. The 300-pound animal never even looked at a person. And after he had eaten – at no charge, of course – he simply pushed through the front door and walked down the street.

Justin always thought it would be exciting not only to be near a bear, but even to touch one. The closest he had ever come to that was at the beginning of the summer at the Pied Piper in Old Forge. The huge animal had brushed right up against the family jeep and grabbed a meal out of a garbage can.

Somehow he felt safe then. But that was when he was with his mom and dad and there were a lot of people and cars and buildings all around. But here? Alone in the wilderness? He looked over at the gashes in the tree again, thinking they might look smaller this time. They didn't.

"What was that?" asked Jackie. There was a noise in some bushes from somewhere out behind the tent – just outside the clearing – just beyond their view.

Jackie wasn't afraid. "If it's a bear, don't run," she said. "Just make a lot of noise."

Then it was very quiet.

Grandpa Robert distracted them. "All right," he said. "Let's wedge the bear canisters between some rocks and head for the falls."

With the food secure some 100 feet from the

campsite, they all took the short walk farther up the Yellow trail.

"I already hear the water running," said Justin. He walked faster.

Nick ran to catch up with him. "I've been to Niagara Falls a bunch of times," he said. "I can't wait to see this."

The trail widened into an open area featuring a shallow pool. To their left, several tiers of mostly dry, lichen-covered boulders and rocks flanked by white birch trees and plush ferns rose above them toward a powder blue sky. Only a trickle of water caused slight ripples in the pool at their feet.

"That's it?" said Nick. "Our camp faucet drips more than this."

"I still hear water," said Justin. He closed his eyes to concentrate and rotated his head, using his ears like sonar to pinpoint the sound he heard. "I've got it." He opened his eyes and found himself staring up into the trees. "It's the leaves," he said. "It's the breeze in the leaves. It sounds just like running water."

Jackie already had her boots unlaced and was getting ready to plunge her feet into the shallow pool. Justin and Nick sat down to join her.

In a moment, icy water surrounded six tired arches and heels and was soothing 30 sore toes. Pounding a rocky trail for several hours seemed to take its toll on everyone's feet, young and old, no matter how snug the footwear.

Justin was surprised how cold the water was on

such a warm day. Before his feet even hit bottom, he could feel his whole body begin to cool down.

Grandpa Robert was spending time with several hikers who were headed down the trail. Justin couldn't hear the conversation, but there was a lot of nodding and not a lot of smiling. *Were they talking about bears?* he wondered. He continued to watch as his grandpa shook each of their hands and then headed back toward him and Jackie and Nick.

"Let's get back to the campsite, everybody," Grandpa Robert said. "We have more to do before nightfall, and I have a great meal planned." His voice sounded cheery, but Justin knew his grandfather. Something was definitely wrong.

Chapter Nine

Backseat Picnic

Dax did not ordinarily let anyone touch her, much less carry her around. But she voluntarily gave in to the young girl with the small hands and gentle manner. Or it could have been the food she smelled on her fingers.

The girl scurried along quickly toward the candy-red van with Dax cradled in her arms. She reached up with her left hand to grab the handle of the sliding door and held Dax rather awkwardly with her right arm. She struggled to get the van open. As she yanked and pulled at the handle, Dax swung back and forth on her other arm like a trapeze artist out of control.

"Samantha!" It was the girl's mother.

Finally the door slid open. Once inside, the girl moved quickly to the backseat where she placed Dax on the floor and covered her up with a beach towel.

The back door of the van popped open. "Samantha," her mother said. "I told you not to run off like that." Then she set down a large picnic basket and slammed the door shut.

Moving to the front of the van, the girl's mother

climbed into the passenger seat. "Here comes your father and brother," she called back to Samantha. "I want you and your brother to behave on the drive back to Lake George. He'll sit in the middle seat. You stay right in the backseat where you are."

Two more doors opened and closed. "Are we ready to go?" asked Samantha's father. "No one has to use the bathroom?" Everyone nodded. The engine started and they were off.

Dax poked her head outside of the towel and looked up at the girl.

"Shhh," Samantha said again. She picked up a doll that sat on the seat next to her. "This is my friend, Dixie," she whispered. "We're going to have a party."

Dax had no idea what she was saying, but began getting nervous when the girl took a cowboy hat off the doll and reached down to strap it on her head.

Sensing Dax's discomfort, the girl withdrew the hat and reached down to stroke her head instead. "Look at all your colors and that black triangle around your nose," she said. "Your face is so pretty."

Dax began to lick her fingers. Samantha giggled."That tickles," she said. "Are you hungry?"

Not expecting a verbal reply, the girl maneuvered half of her body over the backseat to reach into the family picnic basket.

"Sit down back there, Samantha," said her father, as he adjusted his rearview mirror.

"I am, daddy," she said, with her head nearly

inside the picnic basket and the heels of her sneakers up in the air, brushing against the ceiling.

"Right now, young lady. Don't make me pull the van over," her father said.

"What are you doing back there, honey?" asked her mother. "You can't be hungry again. I know it was late, but we just ate lunch."

"Hey, I want some," said her brother. He turned to get in on the food raid.

Samantha slipped down into her seat just in time to cover Dax up again before her brother leaned back over his own seat for a hand-out. She offered him a half-empty bag of chips. Satisfied, he grabbed the foil package and spun back around. His earphones back on, he started bobbing his head back and forth, and crunching away on the chips.

Once she was sure her brother was occupied filling his mouth with food and his ears with music, Samantha opened a plastic baggy, and the aroma of tuna hit Dax's nose full force. The cabin of the van smelled instantly like a school cafeteria.

She took off the sandwich's top slice of bread and used the bottom slice like a plate for the small chunks of fish. "Here you go, kitty," she said, holding out the meal in the palm of her hand. Dax devoured it. Smacking her lips, she looked up for more.

"That's all I have, kitty," Samantha said. "Come up here." She pulled Dax up onto her lap, towel and all, and began stroking her short, soft fur.

The van's air-conditioning made being covered up

by the beach towel bearable. Dax, now a tender bundle of rufous and black and snow-white colors, curled up on the girl's lap and closed her eyes to nap.

"I am going to adopt you," said the girl softly and yawned. "I think I'll name you, Patches."

Then she, too, was asleep.

Chapter Ten

A Change in Plans

Back at the campsite, the three Adirondack kids finished unpacking all of their cooking gear, including the stove, fuel, bowls, knives, spoons and forks.

Nick held up a bowl and spoon in his hands. "I'm ready to eat," he announced.

"When are you *not* ready to eat?" asked Jackie.

Since returning from the waterfalls, Justin had continued to study his grandfather's face carefully, searching for signs that everything would be all right. Everything seemed to be pretty good until he saw his grandfather's expression as he returned to the campsite, carrying just one of their two food canisters from its forest hiding spot. "What is it, Grandpa?" he asked.

"This canister is nearly empty," said Grandpa Robert, grimly. He set it on the ground. "The other one is completely gone."

"Nearly empty?" said Justin. He peered inside the container to see for himself.

"One is completely gone?" said Nick.

"How is that even possible?" asked Jackie.

Jackie's voice dropped two octaves.
"You mean go back and not climb Algonquin?"

"Bears aren't that smart." She hesitated. "Are they?"

Justin agreed. "Maybe someone opened it and didn't put the lid back on the right way." He and Jackie stared at Nick.

"Don't look at me," said Nick. "I never opened it one time. That's why I'm so hungry right now."

"We will eat tonight," said Grandpa Robert. "And we will pack up tomorrow morning. But then I am afraid we will have to head back to Heart Lake."

Jackie's voice dropped two octaves. "You mean go back and not climb Algonquin?"

"I am afraid there is no choice," Grandpa Robert said.

"But we could just skip a couple meals," said Justin.

Nick's eyes widened. "What?"

Grandpa Robert spoke gently, but firmly. "We packed meals for four people to last three days," he said. "Most of our food and water is now gone. We simply cannot stay an extra day. Sometimes things happen on trips that you have no control over and you have to be smart and do the right thing. Like when a sudden snowstorm hits and...."

"It's going to snow?" said Nick, interrupting him. "We're going to starve *and* freeze?"

Justin felt bad for Jackie, who had been dreaming about a trip like this her whole life and couldn't wait to climb her first high peak. But he felt even worse for his grandfather. This was the weekend he was finally going to become an official Adirondack 46er and join the special list of hikers who had climbed all 46 of the highest peaks in the Adirondacks.

Everyone in the hiking party was going to return to Eagle Bay afterwards where there would be a big celebration with family and friends. Not many had thought he would be able to finish all of the peaks. Not after his accident.

"How big do you think the bear was that opened the canister?" asked Nick.

"It wasn't a bear," said Grandpa Robert.

"It was a raccoon, wasn't it?" said Nick, and bit his lower lip. "No. I'll bet it was a skunk. A big, old, stupid rabid skunk."

"No wild animal did this," said Grandpa Robert. "It was a person."

The three Adirondack kids were quiet. It would be awful to lose their food to a bear. But it felt so much worse to know a person had taken it.

"Who would steal food from campers?" asked Justin.

"I told you it was a skunk," said Nick.

"Please do not speak like that, Nicholas," said Grandpa Robert. "We don't have any idea why someone did this."

Jackie walked toward the cooking gear. She sighed. "How can I help?" she said. Then her voice turned positive and strong. "Since we are going home tomorrow, we are still going to have a great time and an awesome meal tonight."

Justin and Nick smiled.

So did Grandpa Robert.

Chapter Eleven

No Relax Dax

"Hey, Samantha's got a cat!" It was a jarring wake-up call by the sleeping girl's brother.

The beach towel hiding Dax on Samantha's lap had slipped to the floor of the van while they both slept. Dax was exposed and so was Samantha's secret.

The candy-red van was parked on Canada Street in Lake George Village. Samantha's excited mother had only begun to slide the van's side door open, and Dax was out the small gap provided.

"Come back, Patches, come back," said the girl, calling after her unofficially adopted calico cat that was now running quickly along the sidewalk. By the time Samantha climbed out of the backseat and stepped out onto the pavement, Dax had disappeared into an ocean of pedestrians.

There were countless tourists in Lake George, especially this time of year. Night was beginning to fall, but that seemed only to increase their numbers.

Dax was forced to slow down and began to pick her way carefully through a challenging obstacle course of multiple moving legs. There were wide legs and skinny ones, some moving quickly and some slowly. Some legs turned suddenly to the right or left and some stopped and went backwards. Dax weaved her way through the constantly shifting shins and shoes and managed to avoid being stepped on, nor tripping up anyone herself.

There was a set of legs, however, she could not maneuver around. Those of a large brown dog which sat with a wide pink tongue dangling out of its mouth.

Dax's hair stood on end in anticipation of what she sensed was coming next. And it did. The large brown dog narrowed its eyes, sucked in its tongue and bared a mouthful of long, sharp teeth. A deep growl resounded from somewhere in the depths of its unfriendly and quivering body.

All of Dax's skill would be required to continue through the hazardous maze of human legs, for now she would need to advance with greater speed and a touch of panic as a dog five times her size was in serious pursuit.

It was somewhat to Dax's advantage that the dog was large and dragging a silver chain attached to his black collar. As Dax zigzagged her way around each pair of tourist's legs, the dog attempted to duplicate her path. The long silver chain whipped back and forth with every slight change of direction slapping people in the ankles, calves and knees. Occasionally, it snagged on someone's leg and slowed the rushing canine down.

Ahead, a small crowd formed a circle around a

gargantuan creature with a green face and green hands that was wearing a dark jacket and pants. Small bolts stuck out of each side of the giant creature's thick, green neck. Frankenstein was out on the town, promoting a local wax museum.

To the right were wall-to-wall shoppes, and to the left was the busy street. There was no way around the mob; and with the dog closing in on her, Dax forced herself into the forest of human limbs. The dog plunged in behind her.

Dax pushed and twisted and wriggled and finally broke through the tangle of legs into the open center of the circle with the large brown dog right at her heels. The towering green monster looked down help-lessly as both cat and dog ran around and around his heavy legs that were the size of two small tree trunks.

The loose end of the silver chain continued to whip wildly and finally wrapped around one of the giant's ankles. When Dax left the circle, so did the dog. And when the dog left the circle, so did the left leg of the green giant. With a collective sigh, an entire section of the crowd moved backward as Frankenstein's feet were yanked out from under him and the towering monster crashed to the con-crete sidewalk.

Dax never looked back and continued running among the wandering humans. She joined a group of pedestrians crossing the highway, then broke from the crowd to dart down a side street toward the lake. She paused briefly for a breath.

There was barking and she turned her head.

The large brown dog had broken free from the green monster, and was charging toward her again.

Chapter Twelve

Camping Under Moonlight

As daylight disappeared, so did Justin's courage.

There were no campfires allowed in the eastern high peaks region, so a simple candle lantern was lit and placed securely on a small rock not far from the door of the golden tent.

The warm glow of the light shone brightly on the face of each hiker seated in the small circle around the lantern. The darkness pressed in to the nearest surrounding trees, but no farther.

Nick tried telling some scary stories, but he never remembered the endings. And although he didn't mean it, they always seemed funny because of the faces he made.

It wasn't until Grandpa Robert started telling a true story about a crew of four airmen whose jet bomber crashed into nearby Wright Peak, that Justin grew nervous. He could feel a tinge of fear invade the pit of his stomach and then crawl up through his spine and exit through the hairs on the back of his neck.

He studied his grandpa's face as he told the tragic

story about the snow and the plane crash and the search for the wreck and the four poor lost men. The flickering candlelight revealed bright and vibrant eyes buried in deep wrinkles. He was still very strong, but he was getting old.

Until tonight, surrounded by darkness and so far from any other people, it had not occurred to Justin what he and his friends would do if anything ever happened to his grandfather while out in this wilderness. Even an extra sweatshirt he was wearing could not hold back a shiver.

He looked over at Jackie. She sat listening intently to the story. Justin could tell she was not afraid at all. He sighed and felt his chest relax. *She would definitely know what to do in an emergency*, he thought.

"Let's tell some jokes," said Nick. It was obvious from the tone in his voice he was ready for a change of subject. He looked at Jackie. "Knock knock," he said.

An expressionless Jackie reluctantly turned her head toward him. She sat silent.

"Come on," pleaded Nick. "I said, 'knock knock.'"

Jackie sighed. "All right," she said. "Who's there?"

"You," said Nick.

"You who?" asked Jackie.

"Are you blind? It's me, Nick!" he said, and began to laugh uncontrollably.

No one else did.

Grandpa Robert had not spent a lot of time with Nick Barnes before, but he sensed more bad jokes were coming. "All right, everyone, let's get ready for some sleep," he said, before the young comedian could get on a roll. "Make sure all food, bug repellent, toothpaste and any trash is packed back into the canister. I will make sure it is well hidden."

"Yes, *all* your food, Nick," said Justin.

Nick was annoyed. "We couldn't have s'mores because of the no campfire rule, and all the really good stuff was in the other canister anyway," he said. Annoyance suddenly turned to concern. "But what if the bears smell food on my breath?"

"So don't breathe," suggested Jackie, with a wry smile.

"Very funny," said Nick.

Glad to be out of the increasingly damp air, Justin was already inside their small golden dome that tonight would be home. He and Nick would take the outer sleeping positions. Jackie's bag was flipped headfirst the other way. She had the middle.

Grandpa Robert would rock in the hammock under a sky peppered with stars. The visibility of the countless pinpricks of light in the heavens was challenged on this suddenly cool summer night by the brightness of a full white moon that was occasionally framed by a growing number of slowly passing clouds.

Once snug inside their sleeping bags, Grandpa Robert bid them good night and walked off with the candle lantern to hide the one remaining bear canister again.

"Let's play something, you guys," whispered Nick.

"Like we are inside a spaceship."

"Good, you're the alien," said Jackie.

Nick struggled to gather his legs inside his bag to kick at her.

"No," said Justin. "This isn't a spaceship. This is an Egyptian pyramid, remember? We are three mummies."

"That's stupid," said Nick. "I don't want to be a dead person."

"Then I suggest you be quiet and stop kicking me," said Jackie. "The bears might hear you and smell your breath."

"You can't tell me what to do," said Nick, "You're not my *mummy*." He tried to muffle a laugh.

"Shhh! What was that?" asked Justin.

"What?" asked Jackie.

"That buzzing sound," said Justin. "There it is again. What is it?"

"I was just unzipping part of my sleeping bag," said Nick. "It's getting hot in here."

Justin sighed. "I don't really feel like playing anything," he said. "I'm going to sleep."

Nick and Jackie were buried in low conversation as Justin was buried in thought. He didn't want to admit that for just a moment he had mistaken the buzzing sound of that zipper for a rattlesnake. And he didn't want to admit that he agreed with Nick, and felt like a giant piece of candy in a package just waiting to be unwrapped by a hungry bear.

That reminded him. What were those hikers by

the waterfalls talking with his grandpa about any-way? It was about a bear, wasn't it? He slowly shook his head. *It is not going to be easy to get to sleep,* he thought, and tossed in his puffy bag. But there was one source of comfort that did come to mind, and it actually caused him to smile a little bit as he drifted off. *At least Dax is safe at camp tonight.*

Chapter Thirteen

Bad Dog

Dax was still in trouble. The crazed canine was rapidly closing in on her.

A black horse pulling a red carriage klip-klopped by. Just before the mad dog could snap at her, Dax dashed between a set of the buggy's large fast-moving yellow wheels. She disappeared into the shadows beneath the coach and then scooted through the rapidly moving spokes of a wheel on the rig's far side.

The acrobatic cat was nearly caught by surprise as a second carriage was traveling directly alongside the first, and she had to pull off the same tricky maneuver all over again. But it bought her some time.

The dog was forced to stop, its wide body heaving for air and long tongue hanging nearly to the ground. Both black horses, both red carriages and all eight yellow wheels completely passed by before the persistent predator could again pick up the trail. Then it was down the road toward the pier and the tour boats and another massive crowd of happy tourists.

Dax remained close to a long line of people and gracefully weaved her way around more sneakers and boots and high heels. Reaching the front of the line, she pranced over a ramp to board a huge tour boat.

Still in pursuit, the dog plowed his way through the line, startling people and causing them to frown and mumble. Much to the dismay of boat personnel, the unescorted dog scurried over the ramp and took off along the ship's main deck.

Dax didn't know it, but she was moving in a wide circle around the entire circumference of the huge boat. No one seemed to notice her, but everyone was aware of the dog.

A whistle blew and then a large paddle wheel, some 12 feet in diameter at the rear of the boat, began to churn the water. The vessel started its slow and steady launch away from the pier and out into the clear blue lake for its evening cruise.

Dax had turned the last corner of what for her had become a floating racetrack, her tireless legs carrying her around each bend and finally back toward the bow of the boat. Behind, but slowly gaining on her, was the large brown dog. And behind the dog were three boat employees, one trying desperately to keep pace while speaking into a walkie-talkie.

The whistle sounded again. As the boat picked up steam, so did Dax. The barking dog caused people to turn and move out of the way, opening up a clear path for the athletic calico who was still leading the way.

On the third whistle, without breaking stride, Dax leaped up onto the railing of the tour boat and pushed off with her powerful legs sending her hurtling in a high arc through the air and out over the water.

People on the pier and back on the vessel gasped and pointed, amazed at the curious sight of a flying cat hovering between boat and land. It was Super Dax! All she lacked were a mask and a cape.

As the fearless cat slowly descended toward the docking area, she stretched out her front legs, and with open claws, managed to latch onto a strip of wood that was the edge of the dock. She made it, barely, and clawed her way up onto the pier.

There was another collective gasp from the watching crowd as another creature had launched from the quickly departing ship.

Like Dax, the large brown dog had charged up onto the railing and lunged into the air.

Unlike Dax, the dog never reached the pier. In fact, he was not even close. Right after leaving the end of the boat, the barking missile dropped out of the sky like a stone into the shallows of Lake George. There was a huge splash, and everyone watched under the artificial light cast by nearby lamps as the animal finally resurfaced and headed for shore, performing a perfect doggy paddle.

Dax was tired. She found a covered speed boat on a trailer and slipped through an open corner where the tarp was left unsnapped. Soon curled up, comfortable and asleep on a padded seat inside the boat, she never heard a frustrated, wet dog howling out under a full Adirondack moon.

Chapter Fourteen

A Rare Bear

"Justin, wake up." It was Jackie, gently shaking him. There was nervous energy in her voice. "I hear something in the woods. Let's go check it out."

Nick was already sitting up and rummaging through his pack for another candle lantern.

Justin slowly rolled over on his back and began to rub his eyes. "I don't know," he said.

"That's a maybe," whispered Jackie. "And a maybe is yes." She shook him again. "Come on."

Nick yelled and threw his pack over Jackie's legs toward Justin. "Something is in there," he said.

Justin sat up and shoved the pack back toward Nick. "Don't give it to me," he said.

The three Adirondack kids scrambled over each other in stocking feet and out of the tent, almost pulling it down around them. There were a series of squeaks and some scratching on nylon from inside their shelter, and then a small, unidentified animal scurried through the door and disappeared into the darkness.

Jackie was the first to silently march with soggy

socks back into the tent to grab her boots. Justin was next and then Nick, who carefully searched his bag in the dark for the lantern again. He found it and lit the small but powerful candle. Light filled the tent at once. "Hey, there's a hole in my pack," he said.

"It must have been a squirrel or chipmunk looking for food," said Justin.

Nick was very quiet.

Jackie was busy pulling on one of her boots. "Ouch!" she said, then frowned. "I think I found what the animal was after in Nick's pack." She pulled off her boot, held it high and turned it upside down. Sunflower seeds cascaded from her footwear through the air onto the floor of the tent.

"Are you crazy, Nick?" said Justin. "What if that had been a bear that found those seeds, instead of a squirrel or chipmunk?"

"I forgot about them," said Nick. "I didn't mean it."

"Forget it," said Jackie. "We don't have time to argue right now. Let's go check out that noise."

Two timid detectives joined Jackie in exiting the tent and stepped cautiously through the forest. Patches of fog made it difficult to see very far ahead. Gathered around the lantern in Jackie's hand, they listened intently for the source of the mysterious sound.

"That's growling," said Nick, his voice wavering. "That is definitely growling."

They walked by Grandpa Robert's hammock. Jackie shined the light on it.

"It's empty!" said Justin.

Low and deep sounds continued to carry through the fog from somewhere out in front of them.

"You guys can go ahead," said Nick. "I'm going back to guard the tent."

"Fine," said Jackie, calmly. "Let us know if you find a bear."

"Or whoever took our food," added Justin.

Nick hesitated. "Maybe I should stay," he reasoned. "Just in case you need me."

Jackie lifted the lantern higher. "I think I see something moving," she said. "Yes, over there in the moonlight. It's huge."

"I think I see it," said Justin. "It's coming this way. Can you see it, Nick?" He turned. "Nick?" His friend was gone.

Jackie blew out the candle. "Hide," she urged Justin. The two knelt down behind the fat trunk of a large tree.

The growling sound grew clearer. "That's not a bear," whispered Justin. "I hear voices."

What had looked like one giant creature far away, moving through the moonlit fog, was actually two creatures moving closely together. As they approached, Justin peeked around the tree and recognized the distinctive stride of one of them. "Grandpa!" he said.

Jackie relit the lantern and the two friends jumped out from their hiding spot.

"You two should be safe and asleep in your tent," Grandpa Robert said.

"We couldn't help it," said Justin. He began to

53

stammer. "We heard noises and there was an animal in our tent and then we couldn't find you and...." He stopped as he looked at a young teenage boy in tattered clothes standing in the firm grasp of his grandfather. "Who are you?" he blurted.

"I heard noises that I knew were not made by any wild animal and caught up to this lad," said Grandpa Robert. "He is not saying very much. And what he does say is not in English. He returned almost all of our food and water, but I get the feeling he'll bolt away again the minute he gets the chance."

Justin began waving his arms and hands. "Are you - the one - who stole - our food?" he asked, as if speaking slowly and loudly while motioning dramatically would somehow bridge the language barrier.

The boy slowly turned his soiled face directly into the candlelight toward Justin and Jackie, and with dark, tired eyes glared at them.

At that moment Justin could not decide which he should be more worried about – a wild bear, or this savage boy.

As Justin, Jackie, Grandpa Robert and the mystery boy approached the campsite, they saw Nick through wisps of fog, standing like a stone statue. His mouth was open, but nothing was coming out.

There was what sounded like a low foghorn, and this time it was a bear, most of its giant 400-pound, jet-black body heaving inside what once was the golden tent. The bear struggled to get free of the shredded shelter and then turned to confront its small audience, while wearing what was left of the tent like a bad hat. One of the wild animal's favorite foods covered its long, wet snout – sunflower seeds. The animal took a few steps toward Nick.

Justin was frozen too, but not Jackie. She was fearless, and with Grandpa Robert, sprang into action, yelling and clapping and waving her arms.

Chapter Fifteen

The Raving Rooster

Dax lifted her head to the sound of snarling, scratching and biting. She looked up to see the snout of a dog with tongue slashing and bared teeth snapping. The animal was pushing into the small opening of the tarp she had slipped through in her search for refuge the night before.

This was not just any dog. It was the dog. The dog that had made her life so miserable in Lake George the day before.

The hair on Dax's back stood to attention.

Now the head of the dog was inside the boat. Catching a glimpse of the cat enraged him. Pop! Another snap on the tarp gave way and one frantic paw poked over the gunwale. Pop! Another snap gave way and a second paw joined the first. Outside, the dog's two remaining thrashing limbs fought for leverage on the slippery hull in order to thrust the rest of its body into the boat and after its prey.

Dax backed away from the mad dog and crouched under a life preserver. She meowed. She would fight if she had to.

There was a low rumbling noise and the boat jerked forward. The trailer was moving. As sure-footed as Dax was, the sudden movement caught even her by surprise, and she tumbled from her padded perch onto the floor of the boat. The trailer jerked again and began to move forward, then stopped, then went forward again.

Other than the noise of the truck's engine, it was suddenly quiet. Dax looked toward the back of the boat and there was only a soft shaft of light from a street lamp pouring into the open corner where the dog had been. The tarp flapped in the breeze created by the moving vehicle as truck and trailer moved out onto the main street. The dog had lost its balance, and was gone.

It was near dawn, and the trip from Lake George to Chestertown took less than half an hour. The truck and boat trailer came to rest in the packed parking lot of the Silver Star Diner.

Dax cautiously made her way to the back of the boat. Standing on her hind legs, she poked her head up through the opening in the tarp made larger by the mad dog. Dozens of hungry humans were already making their way into the diner for breakfast. She turned and noticed a large creature standing in the front lawn facing the highway. Curious, she leaped to the ground and trotted across the grass to investigate.

The creature towered over her, but it seemed to pose no threat. It was much taller than a black bear

Dax jumped up onto the wooden platform
where the rooster stood proudly...

standing on its hind legs, but not as tall as a moose.

Actually, it was a giant white rooster with a red comb and wattle and tail feathers. Dax jumped up onto the wooden platform where the rooster stood proudly in place. The bird was supported by two giant yellow feet, the same color as it's open but silent beak. No danger here.

A large flatbed truck carrying a load of long pipes began backing into an open parking space directly behind the rooster. It backed up a little too far, however, and the pipes cleared the top of two boulders protecting the bird. The giant fowl was struck solidly from behind, just below its red tail feathers, and began to fall forward.

Dax jumped from the platform back into the grass to trot away. It would have been easy to escape, but her feet became entangled in a plastic six-pack holder that had been tossed roadside by a careless motorist.

The giant rooster continued its direct descent, beak first, toward the ground.

Dax continued to struggle with the plastic hoops, but it was no use. Her legs were held fast and she could not move. She rolled onto her back and looked up to see the rooster's wide, white breast, two beady black eyes and large pointed beak close in on her.

Two human hands scooped up the helpless calico just as the rooster's beak penetrated the ground with such great force that the bird's entire face disappeared into the soft earth.

Everyone, including the cook and a waitress, came running out of the diner to see what had happened.

The cheeks of the man who accidentally hit the rooster turned a deeper red than the bird's fanned tail feathers that now pointed upward to the sky. He pitched in with a number of very strong men to restore the proud rooster's rightful place on the wooden platform. The bird actually looked angry as several others carefully brushed dirt and grass from its breast and beak.

The cat remained in the hands of her rescuer. The young man hopped into a sporty red, white and blue van with a group of his friends who were all dressed in fancy matching uniforms. He continued working to free one of Dax's legs from the man-made plastic trap. "We had better get going," he said with Dax still on his lap. "We can't be late for the competition."

The van full of athletes sped off. Destination – Lake Placid.

Chapter Sixteen

Stairway to Heaven

The black bear stood on its hind legs, and like a furry foghorn sounded again.

"Don't run," said Grandpa Robert, firmly. "Stay close together and keep making noise."

Justin didn't have to be told twice, and couldn't imagine running anyway. He glanced at the boy from the forest who looked more scared than scary now, and was working just as hard as everyone to frighten the bear away.

The bold animal finally dropped to all fours and slowly plodded off in the direction of the main trail.

At first, no one moved. No one said anything.

Justin looked at his grandfather and finally broke the silence. "That bear is what the people were talking to you about yesterday at the waterfalls, wasn't it?" he said.

Grandpa Robert shook his head. "No," he said. "They were talking about a young boy from Canada who was missing from his hiking group." He looked over at the boy who had his head down, eyes gazing at the ground. "There was no reason to worry all of you with the news."

The boy shook his head. "J'aimerais que vous me laissiez tranquille," he said quietly.

"Vous êtes égoïste et impoli," Jackie shot back at him.

The boy's eyes widened. He never suspected one of them might actually understand and speak the French language.

"What did he say?" asked Justin.

Jackie interpreted. "He said he wished we had just left him alone," she explained.

"Then what did you say?" asked Nick.

Jackie put her hands on her hips. "I told him I could not believe you brought bear food into our tent!"

"Well, you're the one who dumped the seeds all over the floor and left them there," Nick argued.

"What did you *really* say to him, Jackie?" asked Justin.

She looked over at the boy. "I told him he was being selfish and rude," she said, flatly.

"What a surprise," said Nick.

"Can you ask him why he left his hiking party?" asked Grandpa Robert.

"I speak English also," confessed the boy. He looked at Jackie and frowned.

Darkness was finally giving way to the light of dawn. The air was still thick with fog – and with tension.

"What is your name?" asked Grandpa Robert.

"My name is André," he said. "André Labon. My

62

parents wanted me to climb these mountains – the one called Algonquin and another called Marcy, to see Canada from there. I did not want to go."

"And so you left your group and have everyone worried," said Grandpa Robert.

Nick shook his head. "You were right, Jackie. That is selfish."

"And dangerous," said Grandpa Robert. "It was dangerous for you and still is dangerous for everyone who is still out looking for you."

The boy stood silent and still. After a hungry, thirsty, chilly, sleepless night out in the woods and a wild bear somewhere nearby, he did not seem too anxious to run away.

The Adirondack kids retrieved their sleeping bags that were thrown like limp rags into nearby bushes. The tent was a lost cause. Still they gathered up the remains to carry it out of the woods.

As they finished packing what was left of their ransacked gear, Grandpa Robert was trying to decide the best course of action to take – head back down to the lodge at Heart Lake, or continue up to the top of Algonquin where a summit steward had a communication device. Huge bear prints headed down the trail made the decision a little easier.

"We are going up," said Grandpa Robert as he returned from the trail. "We will turn André over to the summit steward and report this aggressive bear."

Jackie shook her head. She looked stunned. "Do you mean we are going to climb a high peak after all?" she said. Her blue eyes flashed with excitement. She clenched her teeth and thrust her fist through the air. "Yes!" she said.

"We will take all of our gear and circle back around to the lodge on a different trail," Grandpa Robert explained.

Carrying full packs would make the trip a bit tougher. André shared some of the load. The party of five walked single file in the stubborn fog past the waterfall while jumping on small rocks to cross the muddy streambed. After a short hike along some steep inclines and more boulder hopping, they stopped at the Wright Peak junction for rest and a drink of water. A yellow arrow on a brown marker pointed the way and noted the remaining distance to the top of Algonquin.

Nick read the marker. ".9," he said. "That's less than a mile, right? It will be easy from here!"

Justin was not so sure. He turned his attention to another sign that was written in both French and English. He read it. "Entering Alpine Zone," he said. "Walk only on hard rock surface."

"What's an alpine zone?" asked Nick. "What happens if we don't walk on the rock? Do we blow up?"

"You play way too many video games," said Jackie. "The alpine zone is a special place on top of the mountain where really rare plants and flowers live. If you step on a plant, it can take almost forever for one to grow back."

Grandpa Robert smiled, impressed with Jackie's knowledge of the high peaks wilderness. He slipped his pack back on. "Let's go, everybody," he said.

A steep, slippery sheet of rock slowed the hikers down. Yellow trail markers posted high up on trees continued to show the way.

Justin hesitated and Nick almost ran into him. There was a noise in the fog behind them. He wondered. *Was it another wild animal?* He shivered. Maybe the pack on his back would protect him from a rear attack.

A hiker with a fanny pack and an open map moved quickly past them. Justin sighed with momentary relief, but from that point on every extra large boulder in the mist ahead resembled a black bear.

There was another turn in the rocky trail and again it was up, up, up. Justin's legs felt like they were on fire. He looked at André, who still looked very unhappy. Maybe the boy was right. Maybe climbing mountains wasn't that much fun at all. But there was Jackie, still pounding the trail, close to the heels of his grandfather. And there was Grandpa Robert leading the charge, finally on his way to becoming an official Adirondack 46er.

Halfway up yet another steep incline, everyone paused and huddled to read a large white sign with red letters that was tacked high on yet another tree.

WARNING
WEATHER SUBJECT TO SEVERE CHANGE. DO NOT PROCEED BEYOND THIS POINT WITHOUT PROPER GEAR

Justin turned from the warning sign. His shoulders dropped as he looked up at what seemed like an endless trail. His pack suddenly felt twice as heavy. *Can I do this?* he wondered.

Grandpa Robert began to march again, using each rock underfoot like steps to push upward. "This is it," he said, then stopped abruptly. He looked back over his shoulder, pointed upward with his pole and smiled. "Stairway to heaven."

Chapter Seventeen

The Calm
Before the Storm

Dax appreciated being set free from the plastic trap by the friendly athlete, but as soon as the van door opened in Lake Placid, she was off her rescuer's lap and running again.

"You're welcome!" the young man called after her. He laughed and trotted off toward the village's sports complex.

Dax moved from tire to tire sneaking under and around the many cars and trucks that already filled the large parking lot.

No mad dogs or raving roosters or large green men were chasing her here, and she casually spent more than an hour exploring the grounds of her new environment.

She saw people climbing into what looked like a familiar means of transportation – a jet ski – except it wasn't on water. One, two, three, four people wearing shiny red helmets climbed aboard.

Maybe it was a way home. Dax silently jumped in, surprising the person whose lap she landed in. Before the startled rider could tell anyone about her discovery, the vehicle was off and hurtling down a half-mile chute.

It wasn't a jet ski at all. It was a bobsled – on wheels. Dax was riding the Summer Storm, barreling in a bright blue missile down a historic Olympic track.

The bobsled suddenly zigged, rumbled, and then zagged. She could hear two of the humans howling, including the one holding her. She struggled for a view. She had so recently ridden on a kayak on top of a jeep traveling 55 miles per hour – it would take more than a fast, loud, bumpy ride in a metal boat on wheels to panic her. She was much more concerned about the human hands that gripped and squeezed her tighter and tighter as the ride continued.

As the speeding sled came to a grinding stop, Dax felt the human's hands relax and even begin to pet her. Then she felt a firm tug. Something was being placed around her neck. That was it. Time again to run and find somewhere dark and safe. Somewhere to rest. Somewhere with no humans.

She saw it. A white, boxy vehicle with a series of small shelves built into its side was quietly parked behind a nearby building. She picked an empty lower shelf that was easily reached, and leaped in.

There was peace for about 30 seconds. Before she could even properly survey her surroundings, a man in a blue and white striped uniform and baseball cap suddenly appeared, grabbed a handle up high, and slammed the side door of the big box shut.

Was she in another bus? Maybe. But this was cold

– frigid cold. As her new prison began to move, bottles and cans rattled all around her. Dax would be making deliveries – in a four-bay soda truck.

Chapter Eighteen

Islands in the Sky

As the five hikers continued their upward climb to heaven, a bird began to sing somewhere out in the fog.

Jackie stopped. "Listen," she said. "That's a white-throated sparrow. Do you hear what he's saying? It's like, 'poor Sam Peabody – Peabody – Peabody.'"

"Who is Sam Peabody?" asked Nick. Resting with one foot on a sharp boulder, he shifted his pack uneasily and almost lost his balance. "What about poor me!" he said, as he steadied himself. "My back hurts, my feet are sore, and I'm starving. That sparrow should be whistling, 'poor Nick Barnes – Nick Barnes – Nick Barnes'."

The angle of ascent was extreme, and Justin was tired. He had even stopped worrying about bears. "Let's just keep moving," he said. The main thing keeping him going now was the promise of what lay ahead – of whatever it was at the top of the mountain that Jackie and his grandpa were so excited about.

His perseverance did not go unrewarded, as one by one, the Adirondack kids suddenly broke through the fog. It was like passing through the front door of a house to suddenly enter the outdoors. They now stood in the sun and were surrounded by an open sea of evergreen trees that were all shorter than they were.

Each small conifer looked gnarled and twisted, but somehow strong and determined. Together they resembled an army of scruffy sentries, each one with branches that looked like stiff hair combed all to one side.

"These trees look kind of eerie – like they're alive and guarding something," said Justin.

"They are certainly alive; and in a way, they *are* standing on guard," said Grandpa Robert. "They are watchmen reminding us of the unique environment we are now entering. We are near timberline, and then comes the summit."

It was true. Now with a clear view of the mountain-top above, there were few trees ahead. From here it was mainly solid rock face, fragile plant life and wide open sky.

"Look at how high we are," said Nick.

Justin turned and looked out over the crawling fog below him that seemed to form a bottomless pit. It had been impossible for him to tell where he was when all he had seen for the past hour were rocks and the backs of someone's hiking boots marching in front of him. He suddenly felt dizzy and his legs began to wobble. Earlier that summer he had finally conquered Bald Mountain back at camp, but this seemed like walking on a completely different planet. In some ways it didn't even seem real.

"Don't look back right now, Justin." The comforting sound of his grandpa's voice helped to clear his head and calmed him. "Everyone keep looking ahead. We'll move from cairn to cairn."

"Corn grows up here?" said Nick. "That's not such a rare plant."

"I wondered when you were going to start talking about food again," said Jackie. "Not corn. Cairn." She pointed to a pile of stacked stones ahead that formed a short, pointed tower. "That's a cairn. We follow those stone markers to stay on the trail so we won't trample any of the special plants." She hesitated. "And there isn't any corn!"

As the trek upward continued, Justin's thoughts turned from struggle to accomplishment. At places the angle over the open rock face was quite severe. A stiff breeze caused him to lean forward and pull his bucket hat down more tightly onto his head.

Grandpa Robert pointed to what looked like meadows of grass with clusters of long blades that blew and clung in shallow soil to the side of the mountain. "That is golden deer's hair sedge," he said.

Justin didn't look right or left. Jackie helped him scramble over a few small ledges. The only things he watched for were the cairns and the dashes of yellow paint on the rock at his feet that also occasionally marked the trail. He pressed on.

"I see the top," Jackie said. "And I see some people." She couldn't hold back any longer and began

72

to run, legs churning, past Nick and André and Grandpa Robert. She momentarily disappeared.

Justin was the last to arrive at the summit, and as the walking leveled off, so did his heartbeat. It occurred to him his hiking boots had stopped pressing so hard against his ankles, and he knew he was again on fairly flat and solid ground. Like everyone else, he picked a spot and dropped his pack. Then he helped himself to an apple and a drink of water.

Where are Jackie and Nick? he wondered. As he devoured the apple, the cool, sweet fruit juice washed down the back of his parched throat. He scanned the summit for his friends. There were layers and shelves of rock that formed convenient seats that some hikers were resting upon. Patches and strips of plant life were everywhere, even in the many long narrow cracks of the rock face. And here and there, blocking his view, were strewn gigantic boulders that were wider and taller than he was.

He saw Grandpa Robert, with his arm around André, talking to the summit steward who was already on a radio, letting the people below at Heart Lake know the missing boy was safe. Some people with packs and maps and trekking poles were gathered around them, shaking his grandfather's hand and patting the young teenager on the back.

"Justin, over here." It was Jackie, and it looked like she was dangerously close to the end of a cliff. Nick stood beside her.

73

"Look, there is Mount Marcy," said Jackie.

Without his pack to weigh him down, Justin felt like he was gliding as he hurried over to them. "What are you guys doing so close to the...." His voice trailed off as he shared their view.

The fog, like reaching fingers, continued slowly to curl and surround the base of every mountain as far as the eye could see. Not one escaped the vapor's closing grasp. Severed from the earth below, the peaks appeared cut loose and suspended in the air. They were like floating rocks above the clouds. They were like islands – islands in the sky.

Justin felt scared and really happy at the same time. Fear and excitement were all mixed up in his stomach. He decided he was more elated than afraid. Now he understood why his grandfather had climbed these mountains his entire life. And why Jackie wanted so badly to be a 46er. Right then he decided that one day he would become a 46er, too.

"Look, there is Mount Marcy," said Jackie. She pointed to the highest rocky island hovering out on the horizon in front of them.

Then they stood there together silently for the longest time – Justin, Jackie and Nick – best friends, on the edge of the world.

epilogue

Algonquin, Justin thought as he walked from camp to Eagle Bay for an ice cream cone. He was still a little sore from his wilderness adventure and was glad to be home. But he could not stop thinking about the trip. Before the weekend, Algonquin was just a strange name on a map – a new and mysterious place he was going to visit.

Now, Algonquin meant fog. It meant an aggressive bear and a runaway boy. It meant his first high peak and feelings he had never felt before. Most of all, it meant an unforgettable time spent with Jackie and Nick. And with Grandpa Robert. What a party they had for him last night!

He took the photograph out of his pocket again. The one they took of their four boots gathered around the Algonquin summit marker just before they left the top of the mountain. *Very cool*, he thought.

Algonquin also meant one more thing to Justin. Missing Dax. He had not seen her since arriving home the night before and he was beginning to worry about her.

He paid for his ice cream and noticed a loud soda truck pull away from the grocery store across the highway. And there she was.

"Dax!" Justin shouted, and he ran across the street to lift her up into his arms. "I missed you so much!" She took advantage and licked his cone.

"Hey, what is this thing around your neck?" He pulled at a crude collar and noticed a bobsled pin attached to it. "Where did you get this, girl?" He looked around for any suspicious-looking people. "You shouldn't be so far away from camp," he told her. "I am so sorry I had to leave you here all alone and bored. I won't ever leave you again."

Dax took another lick of his cone.

DAX FACTS

   More than 5,000 **Black Bears** live in the Adirondacks. The heaviest black bear ever recorded in New York State weighed 750 pounds! These large, usually jet-black animals can be more than 6' in length. Black Bears are mainly vegetarians and really do love bird seed. Hundreds of people experience encounters with bears in the Adirondacks every year. Never, ever feed a bear – it is against the law. Black Bear attacks are very rare. Like all wild animals, bears are dangerous and must be treated with great respect. When hiking and camping in the Adirondacks, be sure to follow the instructions of DEC Forest Rangers and Caretakers.

 # DAX FACTS

The Adirondack **Alpine Zone** is 85 unique acres on 16 of the Adirondack Park's highest mountain peaks. Real arctic plants grow there. More than 100 plants and many moss and lichen species can be seen, including plants that are rare, threatened or endangered. All are protected by law. Those hiking on these peaks should always stay on trails and walk on solid rock. Never pick summit plants; and if you meet a summit steward – ask lots of questions. For more information on the Adirondack alpine summits and high peaks wilderness, contact the Adirondack Mountain Club at www.adk.org.

The real Justin standing on top of Algonquin – the second highest peak in New York State at 5,114 feet. Mount Marcy is the state's highest peak at 5,344 feet. Those who climb to the summits of all 46 major peaks in the Adirondacks can become 46ers. For more information on the Adirondack 46ers, contact www.adk46r.org. ©2004, Gary VanRiper

DAX FACTS

The **White-throated Sparrow** is a permanent resident in the Adirondacks. At some 7" long, it is a handsome brown-and-gray sparrow with its striped crown, white throat and distinct yellow marking between its bill and eye. One of its songs is often translated, *poor Sam Peabody, Peabody, Peabody.*

About the Authors

Gary and Justin VanRiper are a father-and-son writing team residing in Camden, New York, with their family and cat, Dax. They spend many summer and autumn days at camp on Fourth Lake in the Adirondacks.

Gary and Justin VanRiper on Algonquin Peak – Adirondack Park. ©2004, Adirondack Kids Press

The Adirondack Kids® began as a short home writing exercise when Justin was in third grade. Encouraged after a public reading of an early draft at a Parents As Reading Partners (PARP) program in their school district, the project grew into a middle reader chapter book series.

About the Illustrators

Carol McCurn VanRiper is a professional photographer and illustrator who lives and works in Camden, New York. She is also the wife and mother, respectively, of co-authors, Gary and Justin VanRiper. She inherited the job as publicist when The Adirondack Kids® progressed from a family dream into a small company.

Susan Loeffler is a freelance illustrator who lives and works in Upstate, New York.

The **Adirondack Kids**® #1

Justin Robert is ten years old and likes computers, biking and peanut butter cups. But his passion is animals. When an uncommon pair of Common Loons takes up residence on Fourth Lake near the family camp, he will do anything he can to protect them.

The **Adirondack Kids**® #2
Rescue on Bald Mountain

Justin Robert and Jackie Salsberry are on a special mission. It is Fourth of July weekend in the Adirondacks and time for the annual ping-pong ball drop at Inlet. Their best friend, Nick Barnes, has won the opportunity to release the balls from a seaplane, but there is just one problem. He is afraid of heights. With a single day remaining before the big event, Justin and Jackie decide there is only one way to help Nick overcome his fear. Climb Bald Mountain!

The **Adirondack Kids**® #3
The Lost Lighthouse

Justin Robert, Jackie Salsberry and Nick Barnes are fishing under sunny Adirondack skies when a sudden and violent storm chases them off Fourth Lake and into an unfamiliar forest – a forest that has harbored a secret for more than 100 years.

All on sale wherever great books on the Adirondacks are found.

The **Adirondack Kids**® #4
The Great Train Robbery

It's all aboard the train at the North Creek station, and word is out there are bandits in the region. Will the train be robbed? Justin Robert and Jackie Salsberry are excited. Nick Barnes is bored – but he won't be for long.

The **Adirondack Kids**® #5
Islands in the Sky

Justin Robert, Jackie Salsberry and Nick Barnes head for the Adirondack high peaks wilderness – while Justin's calico cat, Dax, embarks on an unexpected tour of the Adirondack Park.

The **Adirondack Kids**®
Story & Coloring Book
Runaway Dax

Artist Susan Loeffler brings a favorite Adirondack Kids® character – Dax – to life in 32 coloring book illustrations set to a storyline for young readers written by Adirondack Kids® co-creator and author, Justin VanRiper.

Over 60,000 Adirondack Kids Books in Print!

Also available on **The Adirondack Kids**® official web site
www.ADIRONDACKKIDS.com
Watch for more adventures of The Adirondack Kids® coming soon.